Karen's Tattletale

**Look for these
and other books about Karen
in the
Baby-sitters Little Sister series:**

Little Sister

Karen's Tattletale
Ann M. Martin

Illustrations by Susan Tang

A
LITTLE APPLE
PAPERBACK

SCHOLASTIC INC.
New York Toronto London Auckland Sydney

ISBN 0-590-48306-4

12 11 10 9 8 7 6 5 4 3 2 1   5 6 7 8 9/9 0/0

Printed in the U.S.A.   40

First Scholastic printing, May 1995

For
Hannah Vera Natasha Janette
a very special baby

1

Stoneybrook Academy

"Hey! Give it back! I'm telling!"

"Okay, go ahead and tell . . . tattletale."

"I am not a tattletale."

"Oh, yes you are!"

I sighed. I looked at my watch. Then I looked at the fighters. They were Jannie Gilbert and Chris Lamar. They are in my class at school. I am in second grade at Stoneybrook Academy in Stoneybrook, Connecticut. Who am I? I am Karen Brewer and I am seven years old. I like to talk. Sometimes my mouth gets me in trouble. I have long blonde hair, blue eyes, and some freckles. I wear glasses. I have two pairs. The blue pair is for reading. The pink pair is for the rest of the time.

"Are you going to give it back?" yelped Jannie.

Chris shook his head. He was holding Jannie's hair ribbon. He dangled it in front of her.

"*Chris!*" shouted Jannie.

"Hey, Chris," I called from my desk. "That is a lovely ribbon. It will look so cute in your hair. I cannot wait to see you in it."

Chris dropped the ribbon in a hurry. Jannie snatched it up.

"Thanks, Karen," she said.

"No problem," I replied. Jannie is not really a friend of mine. But I do not like teasers. So I decided to help her out. I know all about teasers. That is because I have one brother and three stepbrothers.

It was a Friday morning. The kids in my class were hurrying into our room. I looked around. Behind me, Nancy Dawes and

Hannie Papadakis were sitting at their desks. Nancy and Hannie are my best friends. We call ourselves the Three Musketeers. I used to sit in the back row with them, but Ms. Colman moved me to the front when I got my glasses.

Ms. Colman is our teacher. She is T.H.E. B.E.S.T. (I do not know why I put those periods in there. Except that is what Hannie does when she wants to make something look important. Like this: I.M.P.O.R.T.A.N.T.) Anyway, Ms. Colman is the best teacher. My best teacher ever.

That day, she let me take roll. She even let me put the check marks in her book. Hannie, Nancy, me. Check, check, check. Chris Lamar. Check. Jannie and her two friends, Leslie Morris and Pamela Harding. Check, check, check. (Pamela is my best enemy.) Ricky Torres and Natalie Springer. Check, check. They sit on either side of me in the front row. They wear glasses, too. (Ricky is my pretend husband. We got married on the playground one day.) The twins, Terri and Tammy Barkan. Check, check. Addie Sidney, who was pushing herself into the room in her wheelchair. Check. Bobby Gianelli and Hank Reubens and the rest of the kids. Eighteen checks in all.

When I finished taking the roll, Ms. Colman said, "Class, I have an announcement to make." (Oh, goody! I just love Ms. Colman's Surprising Announcements.) "At the end of the month," she said, "our school will celebrate its twenty-fifth anniversary. We will celebrate for one week. During that week we will have a science fair, Field Day, Switch Day, Jamboree Night, and more." (I did not know what some of those things were, but I did not care. They sounded like fun.) "Jamboree Night will be on Friday at the end of the celebration," Ms. Colman went on. "Every class will perform in it — a skit or a song or whatever. Then the entire school — teachers, too — will sing our school song. Your parents and brothers and sisters and friends may come to see you in the show."

I raised my hand. "Ms. Colman?" I said. "What is our class going to do in the jamboree?"

Ms. Colman smiled. "That," she said, "will be your homework this weekend. Think about what our class can do."

Goody. Easy homework. I thought about Jamboree Night. I thought about inviting the people in my families to see it. My *two* families. I would have to invite a lot of people.

2

Little and Big

Not many people have two families, but I do. And this is how it happened. A long time ago, when I was very little, I had just one family. Mommy, Daddy, Andrew, and me. (Andrew is my little brother. He is four now, going on five.) I liked my family. But Mommy and Daddy were not happy. They began to fight. Soon they were fighting a lot. Finally, they decided they did not love each other anymore. They loved Andrew and me very much. But they did not love each other. So they got a divorce. Daddy stayed in the big house where we had been living. (That is the house he grew up in.) Mommy moved to a little house. She took Andrew and me with her.

After awhile, Mommy and Daddy got married again. But not to each other. Mommy married Seth. He is my stepfather. Daddy married Elizabeth. She is my stepmother. And that is how Andrew and I got two families. Now we live with each family for a month at a time — a month here, a month there. (The big house and the little house are both in Stoneybrook, Connecticut.)

This is who lives at the little house: Mommy, Seth, Andrew, me, Rocky, Midgie, Emily Junior, and Bob. Rocky and Midgie are Seth's cat and dog. Emily Junior is my pet rat. Bob is Andrew's hermit crab.

This is who lives at the big house: Daddy, Elizabeth, Kristy, Charlie, Sam, David Michael, Emily Michelle, Nannie, Andrew, me, Shannon, Boo-Boo, Goldfishie, Crystal Light the Second, Emily Junior, and Bob.

(Emily Junior and Bob go back and forth between the little house and the big house with Andrew and me.) Kristy, Charlie, Sam, and David Michael are Elizabeth's kids. (She was married once before she married Daddy.) So they are my stepsister and stepbrothers. Kristy is thirteen. She baby-sits, and is a very good big sister. Charlie and Sam are old. They go to high school. David Michael is seven like me, but he does not go to my school. Emily Michelle is my adopted sister. She is two and a half. Daddy and Elizabeth adopted her from the faraway country of Vietnam. I like her so much I named my rat after her. Nannie is Elizabeth's mother. She helps take care of the people and pets at the big house. Shannon is David Michael's big, floppy puppy. Boo-Boo is Daddy's fat, old cat. (Sometimes he scratches.) Can you guess what Gold-fishie and Crystal Light are? They belong to Andrew and me.

I made up special nicknames for my brother and me. I call us Andrew Two-Two and Karen Two-Two. (I thought up those names after Ms. Colman read our class a book called *Jacob Two-Two Meets the Hooded Fang*.) We are two-twos because we have two of so many things. We have two houses and two families, two mommies and two daddies, two cats and two dogs. We have clothes and toys and books at the big house, and other clothes and toys and books at the little house. And I have those two pairs of glasses, and even two best friends. Hannie lives across the street from Daddy and one house down. Nancy lives next door to Mommy.

Being a two-two is mostly okay. Except for when I am at the little house and I miss my big-house family. And except for when I am at the big house and I miss my little-house family. But that does not happen very often.

In case you are wondering, the month that my school would turn twenty-five was May. May was also a little-house month.

Seth's New Door

"Snap, crackle, pop! Rice Krispies!" I said.

It was Saturday morning. I had finished my breakfast. (I had not eaten Rice Krispies. I just like to say those silly words.) I carried my dishes to the sink. Then I decided to go outside. I was still wearing my nightgown, but I needed to find out how warm it was so I would know what clothes to put on.

Guess what. I could not go out the front door. That was because Seth was there. He had taken the screen door off of its hinges. It was leaning against the door frame. His tools were spread around him.

"What are you doing?" I asked him.

"I am finally going to put up a new screen door," he replied. "This one is so old it practically fell off by itself."

I looked into the yard. The new screen door was lying on the front walk. I could tell that Seth had made it himself. In his workshop. That is what Seth does. He builds furniture and cabinets and things. Seth is a very good carpenter.

I did not want to bother Seth, so I went out the back door to check the temperature. It was nice and warm. Goody. I ran to my room. I put on blue jeans, a T-shirt, socks and my sneakers. That was all I needed to wear. Then I ran downstairs and outside. (I used the back door again.)

"Hi, Nancy!" I called. I could see Nancy next door in her yard. She was skipping rope. "Can you come play?"

"Sure!" Nancy replied. She gathered up

her rope. We went to my front yard to see who else might be outside. We found Andrew, Bobby Gianelli, and his little sister Alicia (Alicia is Andrew's girlfriend), and Kathryn and Willie who live across the street. Kathryn is six and Willie is five.

We were about to start a game of statues, when Nancy said, "Hey! What are Rocky and Midgie doing outside?"

I looked around. There they were. Rocky was sitting in the sunshine. He was giving himself a cat bath. Midgie was chasing her tail. Then I glanced at our house. Seth's new screen door was in place. I ran to look at it. It was beautiful. But it did not close all the way. Not until I slammed it. Otherwise, it stuck open a little bit — just enough for Rocky and Midgie to poke their noses through. That was how they had escaped into the yard.

I stepped into the house. "Hey, Seth!" I called.

"Indoor voice, Karen," said Mommy.

(Why are grown-ups always telling me to quiet down?)

"But Mommy, look at Seth's door," I said. "It sticks open. And Rocky and Midgie got outside."

"They did?" cried Mommy. She jumped to her feet.

We do not let Rocky and Midgie outside by themselves very often. We are afraid they will run away or something.

Mommy and I dashed outdoors. Andrew helped us bring Rocky and Midgie back into the house. Then we found Seth. Seth looked at the door. He swung it open and shut a few times.

Finally he said, "I cannot fix this right away. I need a special part first. For now, can everybody remember to push it closed all the way after you go through it?"

"You may even slam it," said Mommy.

"We will remember," said Andrew and I.

But guess what. The very first time I used that door I forgot to close it behind me. I forgot the second time, too. Luckily, Midgie and Rocky stayed in the house where they belong. I will remember to close it from now on, I told myself. Then I thought I. W.I.L.L. R.E.M.E.M.B.E.R.

4

The Big Rock Candy Mountain

Sunday was another warm spring day. I went outside as early as I could. Andrew followed right behind me. He remembered to slam the screen door closed. BANG.

"That door is so noisy," said Andrew. He put his hands over his ears. Andrew does not like loud noises.

"I know. But it is better than letting Rocky or Midgie outside," I said.

Andrew frowned. "Miss Jewel does not let us slam doors."

Miss Jewel is Andrew's preschool

16

teacher. Andrew loves her. He has loved her since the minute he first saw her. He thinks Miss Jewel is wonderful. He is always talking about her. And he does everything she says to do.

"Well, we have to slam this door," I told my brother. I looked around for Nancy or Bobby or somebody. I was tired of talking about doors with Andrew.

Across the street Kathryn and Willie were rolling their bicycles out of their garage.

"Hi, Kathryn! Hi, Willie!" I called.

"Hi!" they called back.

Then I saw Bobby and Alicia. Bobby was pulling Alicia along the sidewalk in her red wagon. Soon Nancy came outside, too.

"Hey, you guys," I said to Bobby and Nancy. "Have you been thinking about the jamboree?"

"Yes," said Nancy.

"No," said Bobby.

"Well, let's think about it now." My friends and I sat on our front steps. We rested our chins in our hands. We watched

Andrew and Alicia and Willie and Kathryn.

"We could put on a skit," said Bobby. "It could be about the King of Canada and his stolen underpants."

I giggled. "But who would play the king?"

"Not me," said Bobby. "I would not want to stand up in front of everyone in school without my underwear."

"We could put on a *real* play," said Nancy. *"Little Red Riding Hood* or something."

"I do not think we have time for that," I said. "I think we have to do something short."

"Like what?" asked Bobby.

"Like sing a song."

"Like what song?"

"I don't know. Any song." Honestly. Sometimes Bobby can be a pain.

"Karen? Can we get something to drink?" asked Nancy. "I'm thirsty."

18

"Sure," I said. "Come on inside."

I led my friends into the kitchen. I got a juice box for each of us. Then we headed back to the porch. When we reached the front door, we found Seth there. He was tugging Midgie inside by her collar.

"Ahem," said Seth. "Who left the screen door open?"

"Uh-oh. I guess I did," I replied.

"Well, I found Midgie on her way out. Karen, *please* remember to slam the door shut. It will only be for a few more days," said Seth.

"Okay. I promise."

Nancy and Bobby and I sat on the steps again. (After I had slammed the door behind us.)

"Okay, what song could we sing?" asked Bobby.

"How about 'The Big Rock Candy Mountain'?" I suggested.

Nancy and Bobby hooted.

"No, that is too silly!" cried Nancy.

"And it has the word *cigarette* in it," added Bobby. "Gross."

My friends and I rested our chins in our hands and thought some more. But we did not come up with an idea we could agree on.

5

The Wizard of Oz

On Monday, Ms. Colman talked about our school's anniversary again. "Anyone who wants to enter the science fair must talk to me about a project by Friday," she said.

I thought of something. I raised my hand. "Ms. Colman? What is Switch Day?" I asked.

"Oh, that will be fun," my teacher replied. She was smiling. "On Switch Day, everything here at Stoneybrook Academy that is done by grown-ups will be done by

21

students instead. We will switch around. You kids can be the teachers, the principal, the nurse, the cafeteria monitors, the janitor, and so forth. And us grown-ups will be students."

I looked back at Hannie and Nancy. We grinned at each other. That sounded gigundoly fun.

Pamela Harding raised her hand. "Who gets to be you?" she asked.

That was exactly what I was wondering.

"The grown-up jobs will be chosen by lottery," Ms. Colman said. "If you want to be a teacher or the janitor or whatever, you will put your name on a slip of paper. One name will be chosen for each job. You may try out for as many jobs as you like, but you may get only one. And if you do not want to try for any, that is fine. This is just for fun."

Ms. Colman told us a little more about the science fair then, and about Field Day, too. And then Mrs. Noonan came into our room. Mrs. Noonan is the music teacher. Ms. Colman sat at her desk while Mrs. Noonan stood in front of our room.

"Mrs. Noonan is here to help us decide what to do at Jamboree Night," said Ms. Colman. "I hope you all thought about it over the weekend. We need some good ideas."

"Ooh! Ooh!" cried Pamela. She waved her hand back and forth.

"Yes, Pamela?" said Mrs. Noonan.

"I have a great idea. I could sing a song and everybody else could stand behind me and hum."

Of course nobody except Pamela liked that idea.

"We could put on a play about little woodland creatures," said Natalie Springer. (She leaned over to pull up her droopy socks.)

Nobody except Natalie liked that idea.

"We could sing 'The Big Rock Candy Mountain,'" I suggested.

Nobody except me liked that idea.

"We could write a skit about teachers," said Hank Reubens.

All the boys liked that idea.

"We could write our own song," said Hannie.

All the girls liked that idea. (The boys thought it sounded like too much work.)

"We could sing a medley." That was Mrs. Noonan's suggestion. "Do you know what a medley is?" she went on. "A medley is a song that is made up of parts of other songs. For instance, we could sing a medley of songs about school. Or of songs about animals."

After a long time, our class took a vote. We voted on three things: a skit about teachers, a song we would write ourselves, and a medley of songs from *The Wizard of Oz*.

The medley won. Mrs. Noonan said she would put the song parts together for us. All we would have to do was learn the medley.

"I think," said Mrs. Noonan slowly, "that

the medley will be performed by the entire class, but that we should have three solo parts as well. So on Wednesday, anyone who wants to, may try out for a solo. You may sing anything you like at the tryouts. I'll see you in two days, girls and boys."

Yes! Solo parts. I was definitely going to try out for one.

Andrew's Punishment

In my families, if we have very big news to share, we usually wait until dinnertime to do it. That is because everyone is together then. You can make your news into an important announcement. So that day I waited until dinner to tell my little-house family about Jamboree Night, and about trying out for a solo.

But guess what. Andrew had news, too, and he wanted to say his first. "It is very, very important, Karen," he said.

Mommy looked at me. "Can your news

wait a few minutes?" she asked.

"I guess so," I replied.

"Good," said Andrew. "Because mine is *really* important." Andrew stopped to take a breath. "Okay," he said. "In school today someone did something very mean to me."

This was interesting. "What?" I asked.

"Luke tattled on me. He told Miss Jewel I was splashing the paints while we were at the easels. Only guess what. Luke was the one who was splashing. I never splash."

"What happened?" Seth asked.

"Miss Jewel believed Luke. And then . . . and then she punished me. Wasn't that mean? It was mean of Luke, and mean of Miss Jewel, too."

"Andrew, I am sorry about that," said Mommy.

"What was your punishment?" I asked. It must have been something big. Otherwise Andrew would not have been so upset. I thought of Andrew standing in the corner all morning. Or being sent to the principal. Or having to clean up his whole classroom.

"Miss Jewel said I could not paint at the easels for half an hour," said Andrew. He narrowed his eyes.

"That was it?" I cried. I tried not to laugh, but I could not help myself. "That was your big punishment? You could not paint — "

"Karen," said Mommy angrily. "That is enough."

"But that is not a punishment! Not a bad one. I thought Andrew had to stand in the corner or — "

"It is too a bad punishment!" cried Andrew. "Miss Jewel never punished me before. She was mad at me."

"Oh, honey," said Mommy. "I am sure she was not mad at you."

"Well, she gave me a punishment. And it *was* a bad one," Andrew added, looking at me. "A very bad punishment."

I thought for a minute. Then I said, "Andrew, I guess that was a bad punishment after all. I mean, if Miss Jewel never punished you before." Andrew did not say anything. "Andrew? . . . Andrew?"

My brother turned his head away from me. He looked out the window.

"Andrew, are you talking to me?" I asked.

Andrew stared out the window for a few more moments. Then he said, "May I please be excused?"

"Don't you want to hear Karen's news?" Seth asked.

"No," said Andrew.

Seth sighed. "All right. You may be excused."

Andrew left the table. He carried his plate and his glass to the kitchen sink. He did not look at me once.

"Well, Karen," said Mommy. She smiled at me cheerfully. "What is your news? I am very curious."

I told Mommy and Seth about Jamboree Night and our medley and the tryouts for solo parts. But while I was talking, I was thinking about Andrew.

After dinner, I asked my brother if he wanted to play a game with me. He would not answer me. I asked him if he wanted me to read a story to him. He would not answer me. Finally I said, "Andrew? Is it true that you have worms for brains?" But he would not even answer that.

7

The Tattletale

I knew that Andrew would be speaking to me again by the next morning. And I was right. When I said good morning to him, he said, "Meanie-mo."

"Why are you so mad, Andrew?" I asked him.

"Because you are a meanie-mo."

"But what did I do?"

"You laughed at me." Andrew paused. Then he said, "You think you are so great. You think you know so much just because you are seven. Well, that is not true."

I stuck my tongue out at Andrew. Then I went into the bathroom. After that, I ran downstairs to the kitchen for breakfast.

Andrew was right behind me. "Mommy," he said, "Karen did not hang up her towel this morning."

"Karen, please hang it up before you start eating."

I stuck out my tongue at Andrew again.

"Mommy, Karen stuck her tongue out at me," said my brother.

"Karen!" exclaimed Mommy. "What is the matter? Now please go back upstairs and hang up the towel."

I did. When I returned to the kitchen I slid into my place at the table. I picked up my spoon.

"Mommy, Seth — Karen did not put her napkin in her lap," said Andrew.

I jammed my napkin into my lap. Then I tried to eat a peaceful breakfast. But Andrew would not let me.

"Hey, Karen is putting sugar on her cereal," he announced.

"Karen, you know that cereal does not need sugar," said Seth. "We have been through this before. It is full of sugar already."

I put the spoon back in the sugar bowl. Then I glared at Andrew.

"Seth, Karen is staring at me," said Andrew.

"Karen, are you finished with your breakfast?" asked Seth.

"In a big way," I replied. I stood up carefully. I took my dishes to the sink. I folded my napkin. Then I headed upstairs.

"Mommy, Karen did not push her chair in," said Andrew.

This time I did not care. I brushed my teeth in a hurry. I put on a sweater. I slung my backpack over my shoulders. Then I ran outside to the bus stop.

"Mommy, Karen forgot to close the screen door," I heard Andrew call from the house.

I ignored him.

8

The Biggest Tattletale in the World

*W*hoosh, *clunk*. The doors of the bus closed behind me. School was over for another day. Nancy and Bobby and I walked slowly toward our houses. We scuffed our feet.

"I sure hope Andrew is over being such a pain," I said.

"Why? What is he doing?" asked Bobby.

"He is being the biggest tattletale in the world. He tells on me for *every*thing. Every little thing."

"How come?"

"He is mad at Karen," Nancy told Bobby. "So he is getting back at her."

"He does not usually stay mad for long, though," I said. "I bet he is over it by now."

I was wrong.

"Good-bye!" I called to Nancy and Bobby. I ran into my house.

"Mommy! Karen did not close the door *again*," was the first thing I heard Andrew say.

I stepped back outside. I slammed the door so hard it rattled the pictures in the hallway. One almost fell off the wall.

"Mommy, did you hear that? Karen slammed the door *too* hard."

"Karen, did you have a bad day?" asked Mommy. She took my backpack from me.

"Yes, thanks to Andrew," I muttered. Mommy and I sat down at the table in the kitchen. I did not know where Andrew was, and I did not care. I poured myself some juice. "Mommy, Andrew has been tattling on me for everything," I said. "He was horrible this morning, and now he is being horrible again."

"Honey, he is only four," said Mommy. "And he is the baby in the family. I think he just wants to feel more important. Besides, you hurt his feelings."

"But I apologized to him."

"Well, why don't you try again. I think he was too mad to hear you last night."

"Okay." I was happy to try that — if it would make Andrew stop tattling.

I found my brother playing with his Legos. "Hi, Andrew," I said.

Andrew glanced up at me. "Hi."

"I came to say I am sorry I laughed at you. I am sorry I did not take you seriously." Andrew shrugged. "You know," I went on, "sometimes people say things without thinking first. That is what I did last night. I was not thinking."

"Why weren't you?" asked Andrew.

"I don't know."

Andrew gave me a Look.

"Are you still mad at me?" I said. "You are. You are still mad at me. Andrew, that is just not fair."

"I can't help it."

"But I apologized to you and everything. You are the one who is a meanie-mo, you know." I ran out of the room.

"Mommy! Karen is calling me names!" my brother yelled.

"Oh, go ahead and tattle," I called back to him. "I am going to my room. And don't you come after me. I need to be alone."

"Mommy! Karen is being mean to me!"

"Karen, what on earth is going on?" asked Mommy.

"Nothing," I said as I marched by her. I just wanted to be away from Andrew. If I wasn't near him, then he could not tattle on me for anything. (I hoped.)

I went to my room. I closed my door. I decided that Andrew was going through a stage. I hoped it would be over soon.

9

Karen Fights Back

The next day was Wednesday. I woke up in a bad mood. This was because Andrew had tattled on me for six more things the night before. He would not leave me alone.

But then I thought of something. Maybe his stage was over.

I got out of bed. I peeked into Andrew's room. "Good morning, Andrew!" I said brightly.

"Mommy! Karen woke me up before I was ready!" he called out.

"Karen, *please* leave your brother alone,"

said Mommy. "Let's not start this again."

"I tried to leave him alone last night, and he tattled on me for ignoring him," I said.

But nobody heard me.

I went back to my room. I closed my door. I got dressed in private. Then I went into the bathroom. I washed my face. I hung up my towel. I straightened everything up.

"Seth! Karen is hogging the bathroom!" Andrew yelled.

Okay. That did it.

I stomped to the bathroom door. I flung it open. There stood my brother the tattletale.

"Andrew, quit telling on me!" I shouted. "I am tired of it!"

"Mommy! Karen is — " Andrew started to call out.

But I grabbed him. "Go ahead. Go ahead and tattle all you want," I said. "I do not care anymore. Besides, I am going to tell Mommy and Seth all the things *you* have done."

"Like what?" asked Andrew.

"Like you did not make your bed yet."

"Oops."

"And you did — "

"Karen! Andrew! What is going on?" cried Seth.

By the time I left for the bus stop, I was madder than ever at Andrew, and he was madder than ever at me. And Mommy and Seth were cross with both of us.

"What's the matter?" Nancy asked when she saw my face.

I told her about my fight with Andrew.

"Boy," said Nancy. "I hope you feel better by the time you try out for the solo."

10

The Tryouts

I had been so busy fighting with my brother that I had forgotten about the tryouts. Now Nancy had reminded me.

"Yikes, it's Wednesday!" I exclaimed. "I cannot believe I forgot. I did not practice a song or anything. This is all Andrew's fault."

"Well, " said Nancy, "you know lots of songs, Karen. You even know the songs from *The Wizard of Oz.* Just pick one. You can practice it right now on the bus."

It was true. I did know the songs from

The Wizard of Oz. That was because not long ago my stepbrother David Michael was in his school play, which was *The Wizard of Oz.* So on the bus that morning I practiced singing, "If I Only Had a Brain."

"That sounds pretty good," said Nancy when we stepped off the bus.

At ten-thirty that morning, Mrs. Noonan stuck her head into our room. "I am ready for your students now, Ms. Colman," she said.

Ms. Colman nodded. "Thank you." Then she turned toward us kids. "Who wants to try out for a solo?" she asked.

I raised my hand. So did about ten other kids. (Hannie and Nancy did not raise their hands. I was glad. I did not want to compete with my best friends.) But it turned out that I would have to compete with Ricky my pretend husband and Pamela my best enemy. Also Audrey Green, Hank Reubens, the twins, Jannie, Addie, Chris, and Natalie.

Mrs. Noonan led us to the music room.

She sat down at the piano. "Now," she began, "as I said on Monday, when it is your turn, you may sing any song you like. I just want to hear your voice when you sing alone. You probably will not need to sing more than a few lines. If I know the music to your song I may play along, so I can hear you with the piano, too. I will choose three people to sing solos, and three understudies who can sing the solos, too. We need understudies in case the soloists cannot perform for some reason. All right. Who would like to go first? Please raise your hand."

I wanted to raise my hand, but I did not do it. Instead, I drew in three slow breaths. I needed to be very, very calm by the time I sang "If I Only Had a Brain." Meanwhile, Pamela went first. She sang "Over the Rainbow." Addie went second. She sang "We're Off to See the Wizard." I guess we all had the same idea.

"Who wants to be next?" asked Mrs. Noonan when Addie had finished.

Natalie raised her hand.

"What are you going to sing?" Mrs. Noonan asked her.

Natalie blushed. "Um, 'Rudolph the Red-Nosed Reindeer,' " she said. "It is the only song I know all the words to. Okay. Here goes. 'Rudolph the Red-Nosed Reindeer had a very shiny nose, and if you ever saw it you would even say it glows.' "

Natalie had started singing so fast that Mrs. Noonan could not catch up with her on the piano. "That is fine, Natalie," she said a few moments later. "Who's next?"

This time I raised my hand. "I will be singing 'If I Only Had a Brain' from *The Wizard of Oz*," I announced.

Mrs. Noonan knew the music. She played. I sang. " 'Oh, I could tell you why the ocean's near the shore. I could think of things I never thunk before. And then I'd sit and think some more.' "

"Very nice, Karen," said Mrs. Noonan.

Twenty minutes later, we had finished. Mrs. Noonan was looking at the notes she

had made while we tried out. "Okay. The soloists will be," she said, "Chris Lamar, Audrey Green, and Karen Brewer." (Chris let out a yell.) "The understudies will be Hank Reubens for Chris, Ricky Torres for Audrey, and Pamela Harding for Karen."

Luckily, Andrew had not ruined the tryouts for me after all.

11

More Tryouts

Guess what. On Thursday we had *more* tryouts. Only these tryouts were for everybody in my class, and they were just for fun. They were for Field Day, and they were held during gym.

"Boys and girls," said Mrs. Brown (she is one of the gym teachers), "please listen up. I want to tell you about Field Day. On Field Day you may compete in all kinds of events. We will have sack races, relay races, rope-climbing races, three-legged races, and lots of silly contests. You will compete against other kids in your grade. You can sign up for any events you want, or for no events at all. Field Day is going to be just plain fun.

"Today is your chance to test the events, and to see which ones you like or are good at. Some of the equipment, such as the ropes, is here in the gym. The rest is on the playground or on the playing fields. Feel free to try whatever you like. I will be helping you inside. Mr. Prata will help you outside." (Mr. Prata is another gym teacher.)

I turned to Hannie and Nancy. "Cool!" I said.

"What should we try first?" asked Hannie.

We looked around the gym. Then we looked around the playground. When we saw the jump ropes, Nancy cried, "Hey! That is for us! A rope-jumping contest."

If the Three Musketeers are good at anything it's jumping rope. (Well, we are good at hopscotch, too, but we did not see a hopscotch contest.) We grabbed for some ropes.

"You know you have to jump double," said Mr. Prata.

Jump double? That is hard. Two people jumping with one little skipping rope. Hannie and I tried it and we nearly fell down. We were chanting "Cinderella" and we only got to four before we tripped.

"Okay, let's try a sack race," said Nancy.

My friends and I took burlap sacks from a pile. We each stepped into one.

"Take your marks, get set, go!" cried Hannie.

Hannie and Nancy and I began jumping across the grass.

"Faster! We have to go faster!" I cried.

And Nancy called out, "First one to the swings is the winner."

Jump, jump, jump. Nancy was ahead. Then Hannie was ahead. Then I was ahead. Then Nancy was ahead again.

"Tag! I win!" Nancy had reached out and touched the swings.

My friends and I fell on the ground, laughing.

"This is *fun!*" I cried. "I am going to sign up for the sack race."

"So am I," said Nancy and Hannie.

"Now let's try the three-legged race," I said. "I have been in them before. It is hard, but it is fun."

Nancy and I tried it first. Hannie helped us tie my right leg to Nancy's left leg. Then we hobbled across the playground. We laughed so hard we could not move very fast.

"Okay, you try it with me now, Hannie," said Nancy.

Hannie and Nancy ran a little faster than Nancy and I had run. But then they fell, and Hannie skinned her knee. She started to cry. "I hate this stupid old three-legged race," she said.

Nancy and I took Hannie to Mrs. Pazden for a Band-Aid. (Mrs. Pazden is the nurse.) Afterward, we went back to gym class. It was almost over. My classmates were signing up for Field Day events.

I signed up for three: the sack race, a running race, and the three-legged race. I noticed that Pamela had also signed up for the sack race and the three-legged race. And she was the understudy for my solo part in Jamboree Night. Hmm. Pamela and I were going to be seeing a lot of each other.

Midgie's Adventure

It was Saturday again, another warm morning. A week had gone by, and Seth *still* had not fixed the door. And Andrew and I were still a little mad at each other. Andrew was not telling on me *quite* so much, and I was not yelling at him *quite* so much. But our fight was not *quite* over. So all morning we had run in and out of the house — but we were not *quite* playing with each other. Andrew was playing with Alicia and Kathryn and Willie, and I was playing with Nancy and Bobby.

54

"Karen! Andrew!" Seth called. "Lunch-time."

I looked at Nancy and Bobby. "Gotta go," I said.

"Me too," said my friends.

"Come back after lunch."

"Okay!"

We called good-bye to each other. Then I ran into the little house. Mommy and Seth were in the kitchen.

"What's for lunch?" I asked.

"Sandwiches," said Mommy.

"Make-your-owns," added Seth.

"Goody."

Spread out on the table were peanut butter, jelly, salami, ham, cheese, cream cheese, pickles, lettuce, and more. I began making a fat sandwich. I was squirting a mustard happy face onto a piece of ham when Mommy said, "Where is Andrew?"

"Still outside, I guess," I replied.

"I will go get him," said Seth.

But before he had left the kitchen, we heard a horrible squealing of car brakes

from the street. It sounded like this: eee*eee*EEECH.

Mommy's hands flew to her face. "Andrew!" she cried.

Mommy and Seth and I ran outside. The first thing we saw was Andrew. He was standing by the front steps. And he was just fine. But in the street was a car. One wheel had driven over the curb. A woman was opening the front door. She stepped out. She looked angry and scared at the same time.

"I almost hit your dog!" she yelled.

"Where is she?" asked Seth.

Andrew pointed. There was Midgie. She was cowering underneath a bush near Andrew. Midgie looked scared, too.

"I — " Seth began to say. "I — I'm terribly sorry," he called to the woman. "The dog was supposed to be in the house. Wasn't she?" he said to Andrew and me. He glared at us.

The woman did not say anything. She just ducked inside her car and drove off.

Seth ran to Midgie. He picked her up and talked softly to her for a few minutes. Then he put her inside.

"Karen, Andrew," said Mommy. "How did Midgie get out?"

"Who left the door open?" asked Seth. He was running back outside.

"Karen did," said Andrew.

"I did not!"

"Yes, you did. You left it open when you went inside for lunch."

"But I really didn't," I said. "I remembered to close it."

No one believed me.

"Karen, you have left the door open too many times," said Seth.

"Didn't we say," added Mommy, "that if the door was left open, Rocky and Midgie could escape and they might get hurt?"

"Yes," I said in a small voice.

"You will have to be punished, Karen," Mommy went on. "And your punishment is that you may not sing your solo in the jamboree."

58

13

Pamela

I could not believe it. No solo? I had earned that solo fair and square. And I really wanted to sing it in front of the school on Jamboree Night. But Mommy and Seth believed Andrew the tattletale. And why shouldn't they? I had left that door open a million times.

So on Monday, I had to do something I really did not want to do. I had to tell Ms. Colman about my punishment. I talked to her while the other kids were on the playground at recess.

"Is something wrong?" Ms. Colman asked me when I returned to our room after lunch. She was sitting at her desk. She was turning the pages in her lesson plan book.

"Yes," I said sadly.

"Okay, let's talk about it."

(See why I love Ms. Colman? *She* is always understanding and fair. Not like some people I can think of.)

I drew in a breath. "All right. This is how it started. You know the screen door at the front of the little house?"

"Yes." (Ms. Colman has been to my house several times.)

"Well, a little while ago, Seth put up a new one. Only it did not work very well. It closed, but not by itself. And Seth could not fix it right away. So he said to be sure and slam it shut until it is fixed. That way Rocky and Midgie would not be able to escape. Well, I kept forgetting to close it. And on Saturday, Midgie escaped and she almost got hit by a car."

"Oh, no!"

"But she is fine. The car did not touch her."

"Good," said Ms. Colman.

"Here is the thing," I went on. "This time I did *not* leave the door open behind me. I know I closed it. But everyone *thinks* I left it open. So I got punished. I cannot sing my solo on Jamboree Night. That is what Mommy and Seth said."

"Oh, Karen." Ms. Colman sighed. She looked very sad for me.

"Well, I am going to *prove* that I did not leave the door open," I said. "Somehow. Then I will be able to sing the solo."

"What if you cannot do that?" asked my teacher. "What if you are not able to prove who left the door open?"

"We-ell . . ."

"I am afraid I will have to tell Mrs. Noonan about this," Ms. Colman went on. "She has to know. She will want to make sure that Pamela is ready to sing instead. Just in case."

I scrunched up my face. "Boo," I said.

Sure enough, that is just what Mrs. Noonan wanted to do. She talked to Pamela and me that afternoon.

"Pamela, you should be prepared to sing Karen's solo on Jamboree Night," Mrs. Noonan said.

"Oh, really?" Pamela tried hard not to smile, but I could see the corners of her mouth twitch.

"Mrs. Noonan, I really, really, really think I will be able to sing the solo," I said. "Because I am going to find out who left that door open. Then I will not be in trouble anymore."

"But what if you cannot do it?"

I squirmed. "I — I don't know."

Back in our classroom, Pamela pranced around. "I was just *made* for singing solos," she exclaimed. "My voice can carry to the back of the auditorium. I will be a star."

"You guys," I said to Hannie and Nancy, "we *have* to do something."

The only problem was that we did not know what to do.

Switch Day

One morning, Ms. Colman said, "Girls and boys, have you been thinking about Switch Day? Have you decided whether you would like to be a teacher or somebody for a day?"

"Yes," said half the kids in my class.

"No," said the rest of them.

"Well, start thinking. You can enter the lottery for any of the teachers or other grown-up roles. You may enter each lottery only once, but you may enter as many lotteries as you like. You can enter for the next three days. On Friday, the names will be drawn."

At lunchtime, I sat in the cafeteria with Hannie, Nancy, Addie, Natalie, and the twins.

"Who here wants to be a teacher on Switch Day?" I asked.

"Me!" said Addie, Nancy, Terri, and I.

"Not me," said Hannie. "I want to be the janitor or something fun."

"I want to work in the principal's office," said Natalie.

"I want to *be* the principal," said Tammy.

Cool. Be the principal. I had not thought about that. I only wanted to be Ms. Colman. Or maybe . . . a great idea was coming to me. "I want to be Ms. Colman," I announced. "Or Mrs. Pazden. If I cannot be Ms. Colman then I want to be the nurse. Wouldn't that be awesome? I would get to put Band-Aids on skinned knees — "

"Like mine," said Hannie.

" — and put ice on bruises and let kids lie on the cot."

Natalie wrinkled her nose. "I don't know. You could see a lot of blood, Karen," she said.

"I do not mind blood."

The more I thought about it, the cooler being the nurse sounded. I decided I would try for both Ms. Colman and Mrs. Pazden. (But I wanted to be Ms. Colman more than anything.) Nancy decided to try for a kindergarten teacher or a first-grade teacher, and Hannie decided to sign up for every job that was not a teaching job.

When we had made our decisions, we told Ms. Colman what jobs to sign us up for. Then we sat back and waited for Friday.

On Friday afternoon we heard a voice over the speaker in our classroom. "Attention! May I have your attention, please, students?" (It was Mrs. Titus, our principal.) "I will now read the names of the students who were chosen to be teachers or hold other jobs on Switch Day." Mrs. Titus started reading. Her list was very long. When she came to the kids in my class, she said, "Karen Brewer will be Mrs. Pazden, our nurse. Nancy Dawes will be an aide in Mr. Posner's kindergarten. Bobby Gianelli will be a lunchroom monitor. Pamela Harding will be Ms. Colman." (I could not help turning around and shooting a mean look at Pamela.) "Hannie Papadakis will be a cafeteria worker."

Mrs. Titus kept on reading practically forever. But I had stopped listening to her. I was listening to my friends instead. Some of them were cheering. Pamela was one of them.

"You better watch out," she said. "I am going to be a very strict teacher."

"I thought you were going to be *Ms. Colman*," I said.

"Oh, be quiet, Karen," replied Pamela. "You are just mad because you cannot sing your solo."

I shot another Look at Pamela. Then I

decided to think about being Mrs. Pazden. I would be a very nice nurse. I would be kind to everyone except Pamela. If Pamela came into my office, I would put stingy medicine on her skinned knee and not let her lie on the cot. So there.

15

The Three Investigators

That afternoon, the Three Musketeers gathered at my house. We sat on the front steps in the warm sunshine. A pitcher of lemonade was on a tray. Behind us, the screen door was shut. That was because it was fixed. Seth had fixed it right after Midgie's awful adventure. Now we did not have to think about slamming it. That was nice. The not-nice thing was that I still had not proved I did not need to be punished. B.O.O. A.N.D. B.U.L.L.F.R.O.G.S.

"Anniversary week starts on Monday,"

said Nancy. She poured herself some more lemonade.

"Yup. Just three more days," added Hannie.

"Let's practice for Switch Day," I said.

"Okay," replied Nancy. "Watch me. I am going to pretend I am teaching kindergarteners." Nancy set her glass on the tray. She stood up. "Now, children," she began, "it is naptime. Please find your resting mats."

"Wah! Wah!" Hannie cried. "I do not want to take a nap."

Nancy began to giggle.

"Me neither," I said. "I want storytime."

"You have to take naps!" shouted Nancy.

We were all laughing then, so Hannie said, "Okay, my turn. I am going to serve you a delicious lunch." Hannie stood up, and Nancy sat down. "Girls and boys, today we have a yummy selorction."

"Selection," I corrected her.

"Selection. Um, okay, it is bird's beak stew with molasses."

70

We were all giggling again by the time Hannie sat down.

I stood up. "Okay, now I will be Mrs. Pazden. And one of you has to be Pamela. And you come in with a skinned knee."

"I will be Pamela," said Hannie, "since I already have the skinned knee." Hannie bent over. "Ooh, ooh," she moaned. "Mrs. Pazden, I was pretending to be Ms. Colman and I fell and skinned my knee."

"Here, dear. Let me put this stuff on it."

"OW! OW! OW!" yelled Hannie.

"Sorry, dear. Did I hurt you?" I asked.

We played Switch Day for awhile longer. Then we practiced our medley for the jamboree. (At least I could sing the medley, even if I could not sing the solo.) And then Hannie got an idea.

"Instead of being the Three Musketeers, let's be the Three Investigators this afternoon," she said.

"The Three Investigators? Why?" I asked.

"Because," said Hannie, "we can be detectives and try to figure out who *really* left the door open. Maybe we can get you out of trouble, Karen."

"Cool," said Nancy. "We can re-enact the crime. We will play it over again, just the way it really happened."

That was a good idea, except that we could not quite do it. For one thing, Seth was not home. For another, the door was fixed. It would not stick open the way it used to do. Plus, Mommy and Andrew were busy fixing his tricycle in the garage.

"Well, all right," said Hannie. "Nancy and I will be Seth and your mother, Karen. We will stay in the kitchen and pretend to fix lunch with you. Where was Andrew?"

"Outside," I said. "He had not come in yet."

My friends and I looked at each other. "Now what?" asked Nancy.

We shrugged. We did not know what to do next.

"Darn, darn. Boo and bullfrogs," I said. "What if we cannot solve the mystery by Friday? Pamela will get to sing my solo. *And* be Ms. Colman."

Meanie-mo Andrew.

16

Field Day

I was mad at Andrew. I was mad at Pamela. I was mad about my solo, and mad I could not be Ms. Colman on Switch Day. But even so, guess what? When I woke up on Monday morning, I thought, *Today is the day of the science fair. Today our anniversary week begins!* And I was excited.

The science fair was cool. I had not entered it, but Nancy had. And Bobby and Ricky and Audrey had. The projects were on display in the gym. My class went to the gym just before lunch to look at them.

Nancy was proud of hers. She had made a terrarium. She had planted some ferns in a glass bowl, and she had watered them. She said if you left the cover on it, the terrarium could water itself. Nancy said it demonstrated how rain waters the earth. (Nancy won second prize in our grade.)

On Tuesday, I woke up feeling even more excited than I had on Monday. That was because Tuesday was Field Day. It started off first thing in the morning.

"Who is ready to go to the playground?" Ms. Colman asked my class.

That was a silly question. We were all ready to go. Whether we were going to take part in Field Day, or just watch. Ms. Colman led us down the hall. When we reached the doors, we burst outside. We joined the other screaming, running kids.

Bleachers had been set up at the edge of our playing fields. Some parents were already sitting there. A lot of parents had to work, but some had been able to come watch Field Day. Mommy was one of them.

(Andrew was at his preschool.)

I waved to Mommy. Then I joined Nancy. The three-legged race was the very first event of the day, and Nancy was my partner. We would be racing against the other second-grade teams. One of those teams was Pamela and Jannie.

When it was our turn, Mr. Prata called, "Take your marks, get set, *go*!"

Nancy and I took off. "Faster, Nancy!" I yelled.

"I can't go faster. I will — oof — fall." Nancy had fallen anyway. I fell on top of her.

"Come on! Get up!" I cried.

We struggled to our feet. But we could not catch up. Pamela and Jannie sailed across the finish line. They won the race.

Later in the morning it was time for my running race. Hannie and Nancy had signed up for it, too. We had decided ahead of time that we would run as fast as we could and not worry about beating each other. It turned out that this did not matter.

Liddie Yuan from Mr. Berger's class won the race.

Finally, it was time for the sack race. That was my last event of Field Day. Hannie and Nancy were in that race, too. So was Pamela. When everyone had lined up in their sacks, I found myself between Hannie and . . . Pamela.

"I beat you in the three-legged race," Pamela whispered to me, "and I am going to beat you again now."

"Are not."

"Am too."

The race began.

I jumped as fast as I could. "Do — not — fall — do — not — fall," I muttered as I hopped along.

And then I fell. Someone fell on me.

"Get off!" I squawked.

"I can't!" It was Pamela.

Pamela and I were all tangled up. We tied for last place in the race. We could not stop giggling. I remembered that sometimes Pamela can be okay.

17

The Kids Run the School

Wednesday was Switch Day. That was my favorite day of our anniversary week. Even though one thing happened right away in the morning that I did not like very much. This is what it was:

When Nancy and I walked into our classroom, Ms. Colman was already there. "Karen?" she said. "Could I see you for a moment?"

I did not think this was a good sign.

"Yes?" I said. I sat at my desk. Ms. Colman sat at hers. (Our desks face each other, since sometimes Ms. Colman needs to keep an eye on me. In case I talk too much or get out of hand.)

"Karen, I am sorry, but it seems there was a mix-up in the drawing for the person to be Mrs. Pazden today."

"There was?" I said in a small voice. Darn. Boo and bullfrogs, I thought. First Andrew gets me in trouble, and now I cannot be nurse for a day after all.

"So you will share the job with another student," Ms. Colman was saying. "Jack Bahadurian will be the nurse in the morning. You will take over for the afternoon."

Oh. That was not so bad.

Well, guess what happened next. Ms. Colman sat down. She sat at Pamela's desk. Pamela sat down at Ms. Colman's desk.

"Okay, class," said Pamela. "I am your teacher today. You may call me Miss Harding. I will have two assistants. They are Miss Morris and Miss Gilbert." (Leslie and Jannie smiled at us.) "They will be helping me out."

Miss Harding took roll. She made some announcements about what we were going to do that day. They were not as much fun as Ms. Colman's Surprising Announcements, but they were okay. And then . . . Pamela started teaching. And she really taught us something. She was not mean. She did not try to give us hard tests or anything. Instead she spent the morning teaching us about . . . holidays. I was so surprised. For reading, Pamela read us a story called *Imani's Gift at Kwanzaa*. For math we made calendars with the dates of all sorts of holidays on them. For spelling we made lists of words such as *Rosh Hashanah*, and *independence*. I was almost sorry when Miss Gilbert told us to line up for lunch. (I lined up behind Ms. Colman.)

In the cafeteria, Hannie put my lunch on my tray. A fifth-grader collected my money. And later, Bobby had to tell me to quiet down. I did not care. It was time for me to be Mrs. Pazden.

When I walked into Mrs. Pazden's office,

Jack Bahadurian was getting ready to leave. Mrs. Pazden was sitting on a little chair. "Hi, Karen," she said. "I am going to be your assistant."

Oh, good. I had been wondering what I would do if I had an emergency. Now I did not need to worry.

I sat at Mrs. Pazden's desk. I put on the nurse's cap I had found in my dress-up box. Then I waited for an injured person to come along. I did not have to wait long. A few minutes later, two first-graders hurried in. One of them had bumped his knee on the playground. I put an ice pack on it. A fourth-grader came in with a cut finger. I put a Band-Aid on it. A fifth-grader came in with a headache. I told him to lie on the cot. (I checked with Mrs. Pazden first.)

It was quite a busy afternoon. My favorite part of it was saying to kids, "I am your nurse. What seems to be the problem?"

At the end of the day, Miss Harding dismissed our class. I was sorry Switch Day was over.

18

Pamela Sings

On Thursday, we had a rehearsal for Jamboree Night. Our class had rehearsed our part several times by ourselves in our classroom. And I had been practicing my solo at home — just in case. But now we needed a rehearsal for all the classes in our school.

The rehearsal began after lunch. The classes were going to perform in order of youngest to oldest. So the kindergarteners would go first. Then the first-graders would perform. And then it would be . . . our turn.

All the kids in our school gathered in the auditorium. Mrs. Noonan talked to us. She had to use a microphone so we could all hear her. "Remember, girls and boys. Tomorrow night, these seats will be taken by your parents and the other people in the audience. There will not be room for you here. You will wait in the hallway and in some classrooms for your turn to perform. When it is your turn, you will enter the auditorium through that door." (Mrs. Noonan pointed.) "When you are finished, you will leave through the same door. At the end of the evening, you will all return to the stage so we can sing the school song together. Today, though, you may wait in these seats for your turn to rehearse. Okay, let's begin with the kindergarteners." Mrs. Noonan clapped her hands.

Mr. Posner's kindergarten class filed onto the stage. They recited a poem about an elephant and a telephone. It was a funny poem, and one of the kindergarteners kept giggling. He could not stop. Soon the whole class was giggling.

"Calm down, please," Mrs. Noonan kept calling out.

After Mr. Posner's class had finished, the other kindergarten class sang a song. The first-grade classes put on skits. Finally Mrs. Noonan said, "Okay, Ms. Colman's class is next."

We scrambled for the stage. As I hurried by Mrs. Noonan, she caught my arm. "Karen? Do you think you will be able to sing your solo tomorrow?" she asked.

I puffed out my chest. "Of course," I replied.

"You mean your parents found out who left the door open?"

"Well . . . no," I admitted. "But I am sure — " I paused because I noticed Pamela standing nearby. She was listening carefully to us. "I am sure we will find out who did it. And I will be able to sing."

Mrs. Noonan frowned. But all she said was, "All right."

A few minutes later, my classmates and I began to sing. We were standing in three rows. We tried to smile and look happy. " 'Somewhere over the rainbow,' " we sang. After a few more bars, Audrey sang her solo. Then our class sang again.

My solo was coming soon. I held my breath. I let it out. " 'We're off to see the wizard, the wonderful wizard of Oz. We hear he is a whiz of a wiz if ever a wiz there was,' " I sang.

When I finished my solo, my classmates started to sing again. But Mrs. Noonan stopped them. "Pamela, could you please try the solo now?" she asked. "You better rehearse it, too."

I shot a Look at Pamela. She was grinning back at me. "Of course, Mrs. Noonan," she said sweetly. But then she calmed down. By the time she began to sing, she looked almost shy. When she finished, she said softly, "How did I do?"

"You did just fine," Mrs. Noonan replied. She smiled.

The rehearsal went on. The other classes sang more songs, recited more poems, and put on more skits. Kids forgot their lines. They mixed up words. One boy got scared and began to cry.

"This is *awful*," I whispered to Nancy.

But you know what Mrs. Noonan said to us? She said, "Bad rehearsal, good performance. You will be fine tomorrow night."

19

Andrew Tells the Truth

After school that day, Nancy came over to the little house. A bunch of kids were playing outside. Nancy looked at them. Then she looked at me. "We better practice for tomorrow night," she said.

But I did not want to practice (especially if I could not sing my solo). And I did want to play. So I said, "Remember what Mrs. Noonan told us? She said not to worry about Jamboree Night. We will be fine. Come on. Let's try jumping double. I will get my jump rope."

Nancy and I jumped rope. Bobby and Willie rode their bikes. Kathryn helped Alicia play hopscotch. And Andrew rode his toy tractor with the big rubber tires up and down the sidewalk in front of our house.

Nancy and I had reached thirty-one in "Cinderella" when we heard a shout. "Hey!" said a man's voice.

It was Mr. Drucker. I looked at Nancy in surprise. Mr. Drucker lives across the street, next to Kathryn and Willie. He is usually a very nice person. Now he sounded cross.

"Andrew Brewer!" called Mr. Drucker. "Look what you did! Your tractor left tire marks on my lawn. Right here by the driveway."

All us kids ran across the street to peer at the ruined lawn.

"But — " I started to say.

"You really must be more careful, Andrew," scolded Mr. Drucker.

Andrew's lower lip was trembling. "I didn't do it," he whispered.

"He really did not do it, Mr. Drucker," I said. "He is not allowed to ride his tractor across the street. Besides, the garbage truck was here a few minutes ago. I think the garbage truck did it."

"Oh, my," said Mr. Drucker. "I am very sorry, Andrew."

Mr. Drucker went inside then, and my friends and I went back to my yard. But Andrew was crying. Loudly.

Mommy stepped onto the front porch. "What is the matter?" she asked.

I told her about Mr. Drucker.

"Why are you still crying, Andrew?" Mommy wanted to know.

"Because — because Karen told Mr. Drucker the truth about me. But I did not tell you the truth about Karen."

"What?" said Mommy.

"I was the one who left the door open," said Andrew. "I let Midgie out. Then I got

Karen in trouble, and now Karen is sticking up for me."

"*You* let Midgie out?" said Mommy and I at the same time.

Andrew nodded. "Everyone had gone inside for lunch. I came in after you, but I could not find my best dinosaur. So I went back out to look for it. And that was when I left the door open. But I said Karen did it because I was mad at her."

"Andrew," said Mommy, "you know that was wrong, don't you?"

Andrew nodded. His lip was trembling again. I almost felt sorry for him.

"Do you have anything to say to Karen?" Mommy asked Andrew.

"I am very, very, very, very, very, very sorry," said my little brother.

"That is all — " I started to say. Then I stopped. I realized I did not mean that. What Andrew had done was not all right. "I accept your apology," I said to him in my best grown-up voice.

"Okay," said Andrew.

Mommy and Seth gave Andrew a Very Big Punishment. They pointed out that he had put Midgie in danger, he had lied, and he had gotten me in trouble. Andrew had to stay in his room for an hour to think about what he had done. And he could not watch TV for a week.

"Karen," Mommy said later, "I am sorry Seth and I did not believe you. I guess we were upset about Midgie. But we should have listened to you. We are taking back your punishment, of course. I will call Ms. Colman to tell her you may sing your solo. I hope you can forgive Seth and me.

I forgave them. And I told them I loved them.

20

Jamboree Night

"Shhh! Shhh!" I said.

"Quiet, people!" said Ms. Colman softly.

It was Friday night. It was Jamboree Night. In the auditorium, Mr. Posner's kindergarteners were reciting their poem. "Once there was an elephant," they said, "who tried to use the telephant."

In the hallway, my classmates and I were waiting for our turn onstage. The first-graders were there, too, and the other kindergarten class. The older kids were waiting in classrooms.

I could hear the people in the auditorium laughing at the funny poem. Then I heard them clapping. I thought about the people in my two families. They were all there. Mommy and Seth and Daddy and Elizabeth and Nannie and my brothers and sisters. They were probably clapping with everybody else. I was glad they had come to Jamboree Night.

Nancy nudged me. "Isn't it great about your solo, Karen?" she whispered.

I grinned. "I am *so* excited," I said. (I was nervous, too.)

Hannie looked at me slyly. "Fake out on Pamela," she said.

Nancy giggled. I giggled a little, too. But I felt funny. I had glanced at Pamela a few times while we waited in the hallway. Pamela looked very disappointed. I thought about the day before when she had rehearsed the solo. She had probably told her family that she would be singing it tonight. And they must have been very proud of her.

"Just a second," I said to my friends. "I will be right back."

I left Hannie and Nancy. I made my way to Pamela. "Can I talk to you?" I asked her. "It is important."

Pamela and I talked for a few minutes. Then we talked to Ms. Colman. When we finished, I went back to my friends.

"What did you do?" Hannie whispered.

"You'll find out," I replied.

The kindergarteners finished performing. Then the first-graders performed. Finally I heard Ms. Colman say, "Okay, class. It is our turn."

My classmates and I lined up. We filed into the auditorium. To our left were the people in the audience. To our right was the stage. We walked onto the stage the way Mrs. Noonan had told us to.

When we were standing in our rows, Mrs. Noonan turned to the audience. "This is Ms. Colman's second-grade class," she announced. "They are going to sing a medley of songs from *The Wizard of Oz*."

I drew in a breath. I tried to make the butterflies in my stomach calm down. Relax, relax, I said to myself.

Mrs. Noonan began playing the piano. My friends and I began singing. My butterflies flew away.

When it was time for my solo, I looked over at Pamela. I nodded to her. Then I sang, "We're off to see the wizard, the wonderful Wizard of Oz."

Then Pamela sang, "We hear he is a whiz of a wiz, if ever a wiz there was."

We traded lines that way until the solo part was finished. Then Pamela and I smiled at each other. We had *both* been able to sing by ourselves. I thought that was only fair.

When my classmates and I finished our medley, the audience clapped loudly. And I heard a long, loud whistle. (I think it was Sam.) We left the auditorium. We waited for the other classes to perform. At long last we were standing on the stage *again* — with every single student in Stoneybrook

Academy. We sang our school song. The teachers and even some of the people in the audience sang with us. When Mrs. Noonan sounded the last note on the piano, everyone cheered. My friends and I jumped up and down. The Three Musketeers hugged each other. Jamboree Night was over. Our anniversary week was over. I felt tired and happy.

"I guess Mrs. Noonan was right," Nancy said to me.

"About what?" I asked.

"Bad rehearsal, good performance."

"I'll say," I replied.

And then I went looking for my two families.

About the Author

ANN M. MARTIN lives in New York City and loves animals, especially cats. She has two cats of her own, Mouse and Rosie.

Other books by Ann M. Martin that you might enjoy are *Stage Fright*; *Me and Katie (the Pest)*; and the books in *The Baby-sitters Club* series.

Ann likes ice cream and *I Love Lucy*. And she has her own little sister, whose name is Jane.

Little Sister

Don't miss #62

KAREN'S NEW BIKE

A salesperson came right over. "Hi, I'm Mike. Let me fix a few things."

Mike raised the seat. Then he pointed it a different way. He unscrewed the handlebars and moved that, too. I sat on the bike.

"It is perfect," I said. "Thank you!"

"Are you happy with it? Is it the one you want?" asked Daddy.

I got up and looked at the bike. It was pink and purple just like I wanted. But then the bike next to it caught my eye. It was a blue and red Cougar Cat. It was a pretty bike, too. Oh, no. Which one? Pink and purple. Blue and red. Pink. Purple. Blue. Red.

Finally I put my hand on the handlebars of the pink and purple bike.

"This is definitely the one I want," I said.

LITTLE 🍎 APPLE®

BABY·SITTERS

Little Sister™

by Ann M. Martin, author of *The Baby-sitters Club*®

☐ MQ44300-3	#1	Karen's Witch	$2.95
☐ MQ44259-7	#2	Karen's Roller Skates	$2.95
☐ MQ44299-7	#3	Karen's Worst Day	$2.95
☐ MQ44264-3	#4	Karen's Kittycat Club	$2.95
☐ MQ44258-9	#5	Karen's School Picture	$2.95
☐ MQ44298-8	#6	Karen's Little Sister	$2.95
☐ MQ44257-0	#7	Karen's Birthday	$2.95
☐ MQ42670-2	#8	Karen's Haircut	$2.95
☐ MQ43652-X	#9	Karen's Sleepover	$2.95
☐ MQ43651-1	#10	Karen's Grandmothers	$2.95
☐ MQ43650-3	#11	Karen's Prize	$2.95
☐ MQ43649-X	#12	Karen's Ghost	$2.95
☐ MQ43648-1	#13	Karen's Surprise	$2.75
☐ MQ43646-5	#14	Karen's New Year	$2.75
☐ MQ43645-7	#15	Karen's in Love	$2.75
☐ MQ43644-9	#16	Karen's Goldfish	$2.75
☐ MQ43643-0	#17	Karen's Brothers	$2.75
☐ MQ43642-2	#18	Karen's Home-Run	$2.75
☐ MQ43641-4	#19	Karen's Good-Bye	$2.95
☐ MQ44823-4	#20	Karen's Carnival	$2.75
☐ MQ44824-2	#21	Karen's New Teacher	$2.95
☐ MQ44833-1	#22	Karen's Little Witch	$2.95
☐ MQ44832-3	#23	Karen's Doll	$2.95
☐ MQ44859-5	#24	Karen's School Trip	$2.95
☐ MQ44831-5	#25	Karen's Pen Pal	$2.95
☐ MQ44830-7	#26	Karen's Ducklings	$2.75
☐ MQ44829-3	#27	Karen's Big Joke	$2.95
☐ MQ44828-5	#28	Karen's Tea Party	$2.95

More Titles... ➡

Now THE BABY-SITTERS CLUB®

★ is a Video Club too! ★